**This book is to be returned on or before
the last date stamped below.**

LIBREX

A Red Fox Book

Published by Random House Children's Books
20 Vauxhall Bridge Road, London SW1V 2SA

A division of Random House UK Ltd
London Melbourne Sydney Auckland
Johannesburg and agencies throughout the world

Copyright © Deborah King 1993

1 3 5 7 9 10 8 6 4 2

First published in Great Britain by Hutchinson Children's Books 1993

Red Fox edition 1995

Printed and bound in China

RANDOM HOUSE UK Limited Reg. No. 954009

ISBN 0 09 950131 7

And from high in the branches,
two magpies flew up and up,
their wings brilliant against the
blue sky.

Cautiously, the black and white cat crept out into the countryside. She hid in the long grass.

Even the insects are more colourful than me, she thought sadly.